Alicia's Best Friends

Lisa Jahn-Clough

Houghton Mifflin Company Boston 2003

Walter Lorraine Books

For my best friends
(you know who you are)

Walter Lorraine ⟨wʁ⟩ Books

www.houghtonmifflinbooks.com

Library of Congress Cataloging-in-Publication Data
Jahn-Clough, Lisa.
Alicia's best friends / by Lisa Jahn-Clough.
p. cm.
"Walter Lorraine Books."
Summary: When her friends want Alicia to choose which
one of them is the best, she has problems.
ISBN 0-618-23951-0
[1. Best friends—Fiction. 2. Friendship—Fiction.] I. Title.
PZ7.J153536 An 2003
[E]—dc21
2002009341

Printed in Singapore
TWP 10 9 8 7 6 5 4 3 2 1

I am Alicia. This is my dog, Neptune.
I have four friends.
My friends are great.

Mitchell is an excellent soccer player.

Charlotte paints beautiful pictures.

Henry tells the funniest jokes.

Lucy finds the most interesting bugs.

I like my friends so much,
I decide to have a party.
I hand out invitations one by one.

6

"What kind of party is this?" Mitchell asks.
"It's a best friends party," I say.
"But who is your best friend?" Charlotte asks.
"Yeah, who?" Henry says.
"You have to pick," says Lucy.
"Woof!" says Neptune.

"But I don't know who to pick," I say.

11

"Pick me," says Mitchell.
"Pick me," says Charlotte.
"Pick me," says Henry.
"Pick me," says Lucy.
"Woof!" says Neptune.

I pick Mitchell, but I miss Charlotte.

So I pick Charlotte, but I miss Henry.

15

When I pick Henry, I miss Lucy.

And when I pick Lucy, I miss Mitchell again.

"I give up!" I shout.
Neptune and I go off by ourselves.

We play tug of war.

We turn cartwheels
and roll down the hill.

"I pick you, Neptune!" I say.

But when I kick the ball, Neptune walks away.

I draw a picture in the dirt. Neptune ruins it.

I tell a joke. Neptune doesn't laugh.

I chase a fly. Neptune eats it.

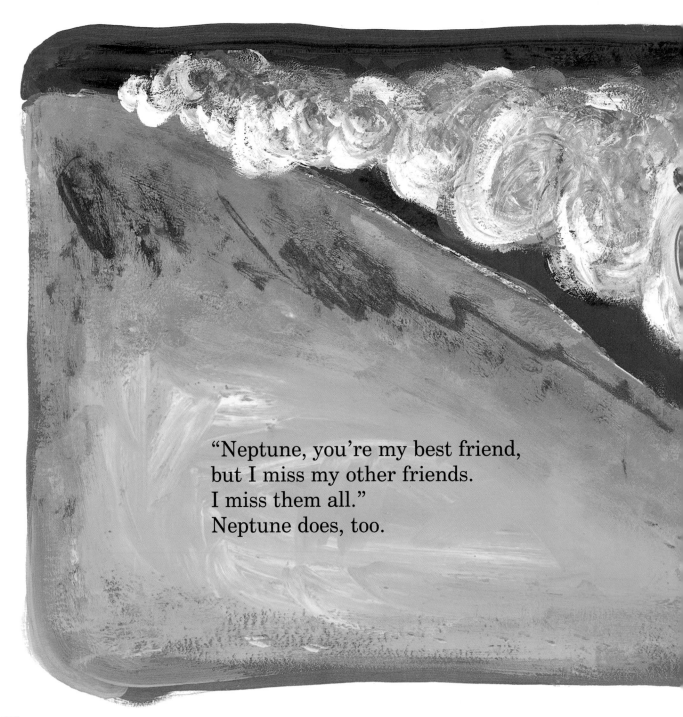

"Neptune, you're my best friend,
but I miss my other friends.
I miss them all."
Neptune does, too.

And suddenly I know.
"Mitchell! Charlotte!
Henry! Lucy!" I call.
"I know who to pick!"

"Who?" they all ask.

"Mitchell," I say, "is my best soccer friend.
Charlotte is my best painting friend.
Henry is my best funny friend.
Lucy is my best bug-finding friend.
And Neptune is my best dog friend!"

I am Alicia. I have five friends.
My friends are the best!